LEVEL 1

THIS IS SPIDER-MAN

By Thomas Macri

Illustrated by Todd Nauck *and* Hi-Fi Design

Based on the Marvel comic book series The Amazing Spider-Man

ABDO
Spotlight

New York

WWW.ABDOPUBLISHING.COM

Reinforced library bound edition published in 2015 by Spotlight, a division of ABDO
PO Box 398166, Minneapolis, Minnesota 55439. Spotlight produces high-quality
reinforced library bound editions for schools and libraries. Published by Marvel Press,
an imprint of Disney Book Group.

Printed in the United States of America, North Mankato, Minnesota.
052014
072014

THIS BOOK CONTAINS
RECYCLED MATERIALS

marvelkids.com
TM & © 2012 Marvel & Subs.

LIBRARY OF CONGRESS CATALOGING-IN-PUBLICATION DATA

This title was previously cataloged with the following information:

Macri, Thomas.
This is Spider-Man / by Thomas Macri ; illustrated by Todd Nauck and Hi-Fi Design.
  p. cm. -- (World of reading. Level 1)
Summary: Introduces the superhero Spider-Man, explaining what makes him special.
1. Spider-Man (Fictitious characters)--Juvenile fiction. 2. Superheroes--Juvenile fiction.
I. Nauck, Todd, ill. II. Hi-Fi Colour Design, ill. III. Title. IV. Series.
PZ7.M24731Tk 2012
[Fic]--dc23

2012288828

978-1-61479-255-0   (Reinforced Library Bound Edition)

Spotlight
A Division of ABDO
www.abdopublishing.com

This is Peter.

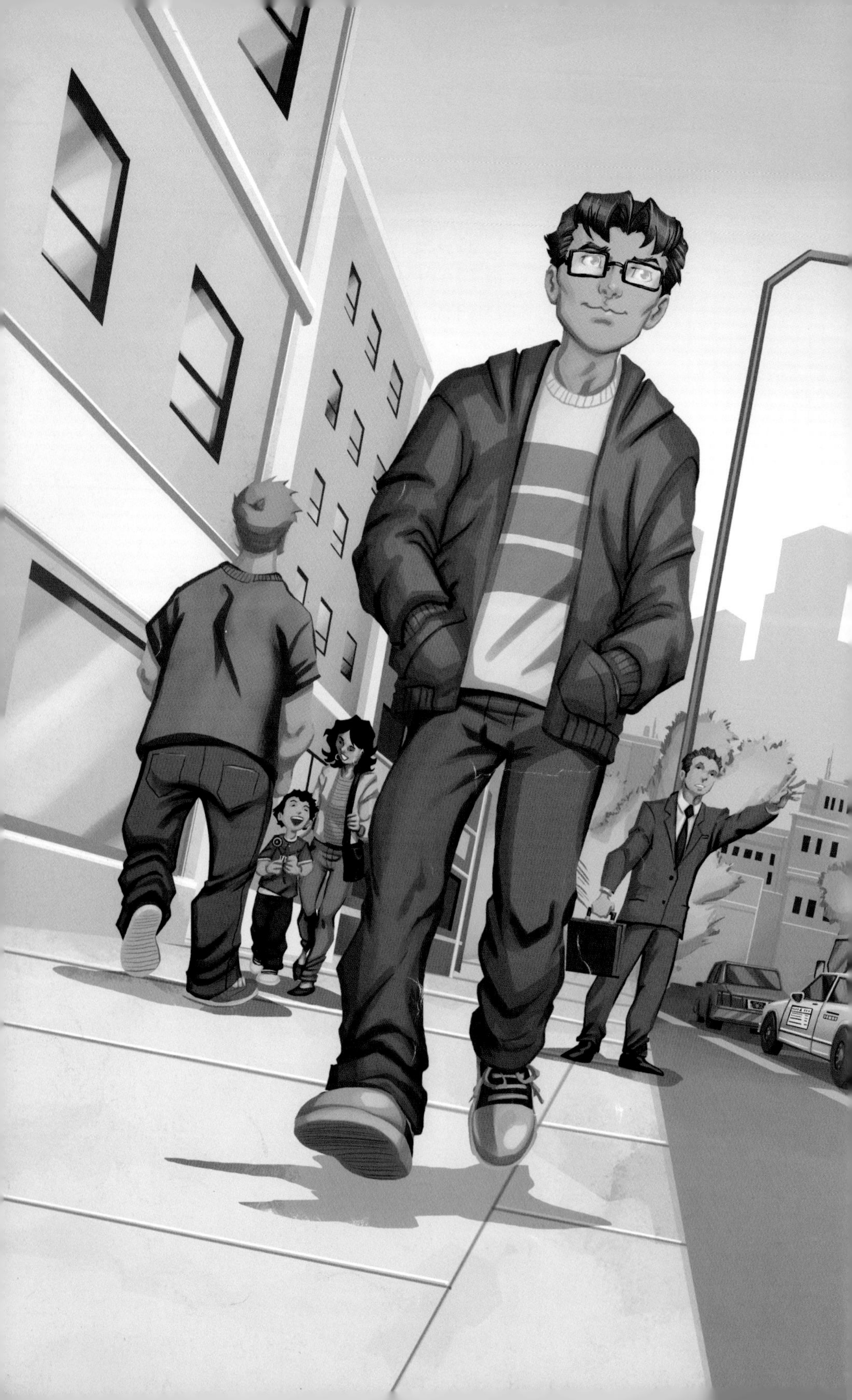

Peter lives in Queens.
Queens is in
New York City.

Peter lives with his aunt.
Her name is Aunt May.

Peter loves Aunt May
very much.

Peter is a student.

He goes to high school.

Peter loves school.
He loves math.

He loves science.

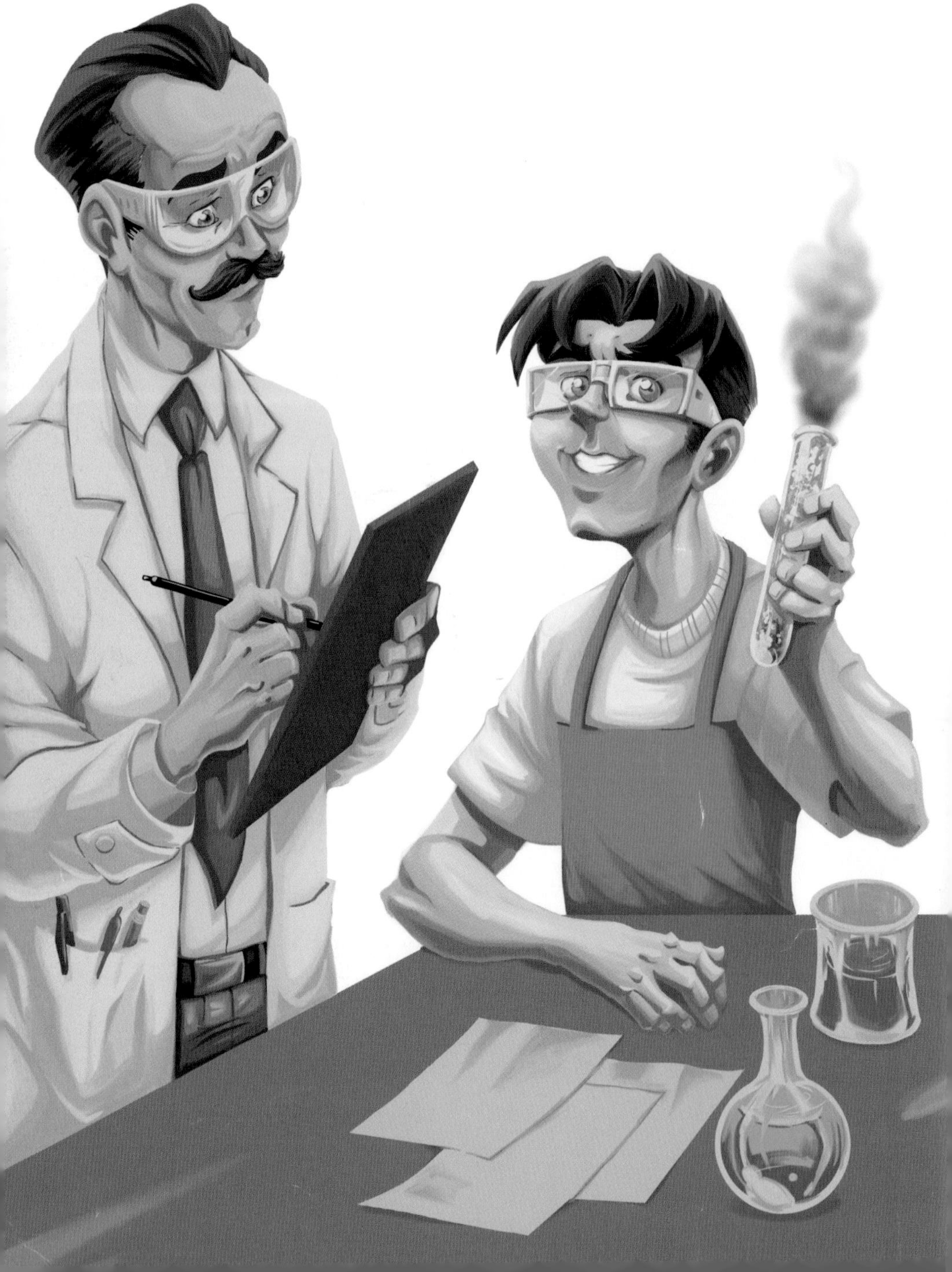

Some kids at school are
not nice to Peter.

They push him.
They make fun of him.

Peter does not care.

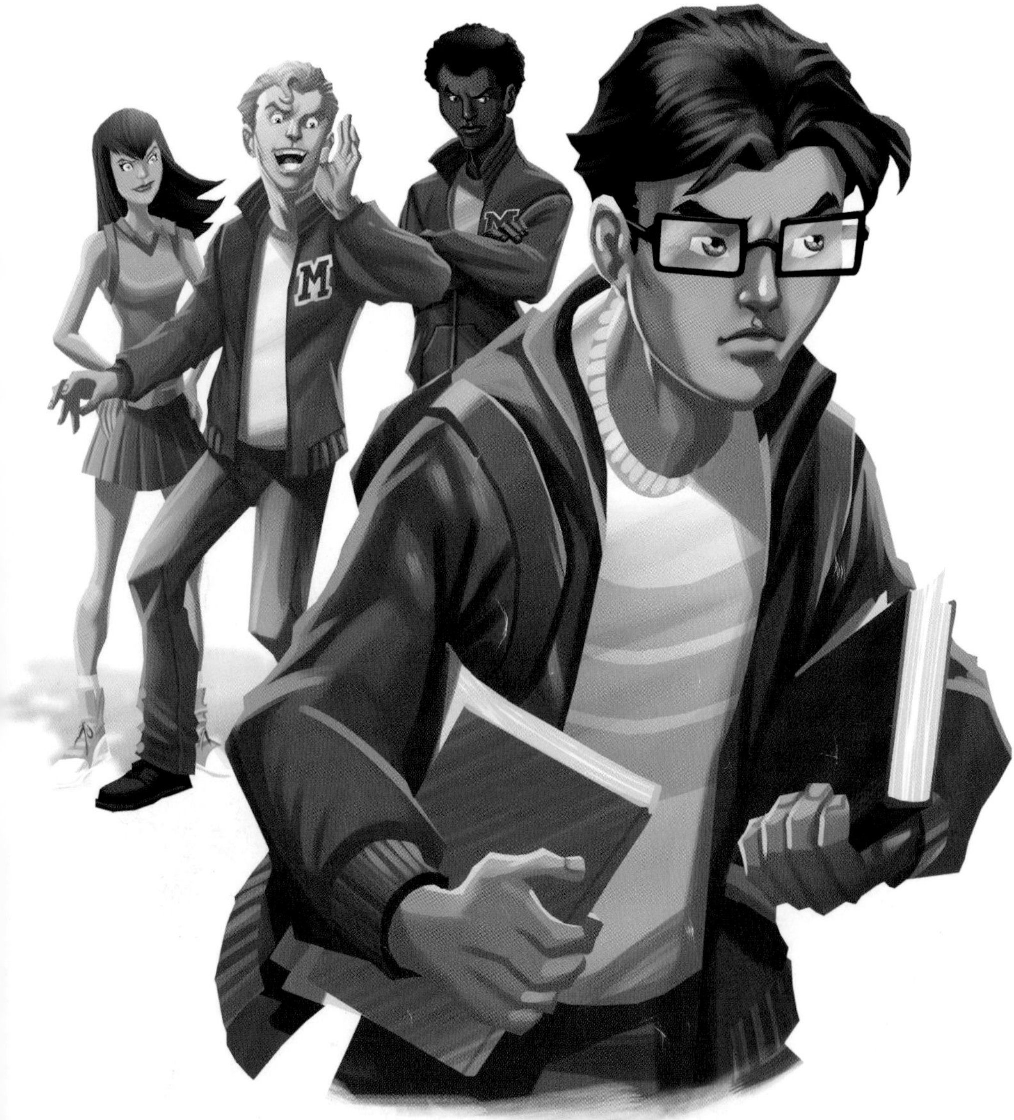

M
M

At home, no one makes fun
of Peter.

Peter has a super secret.

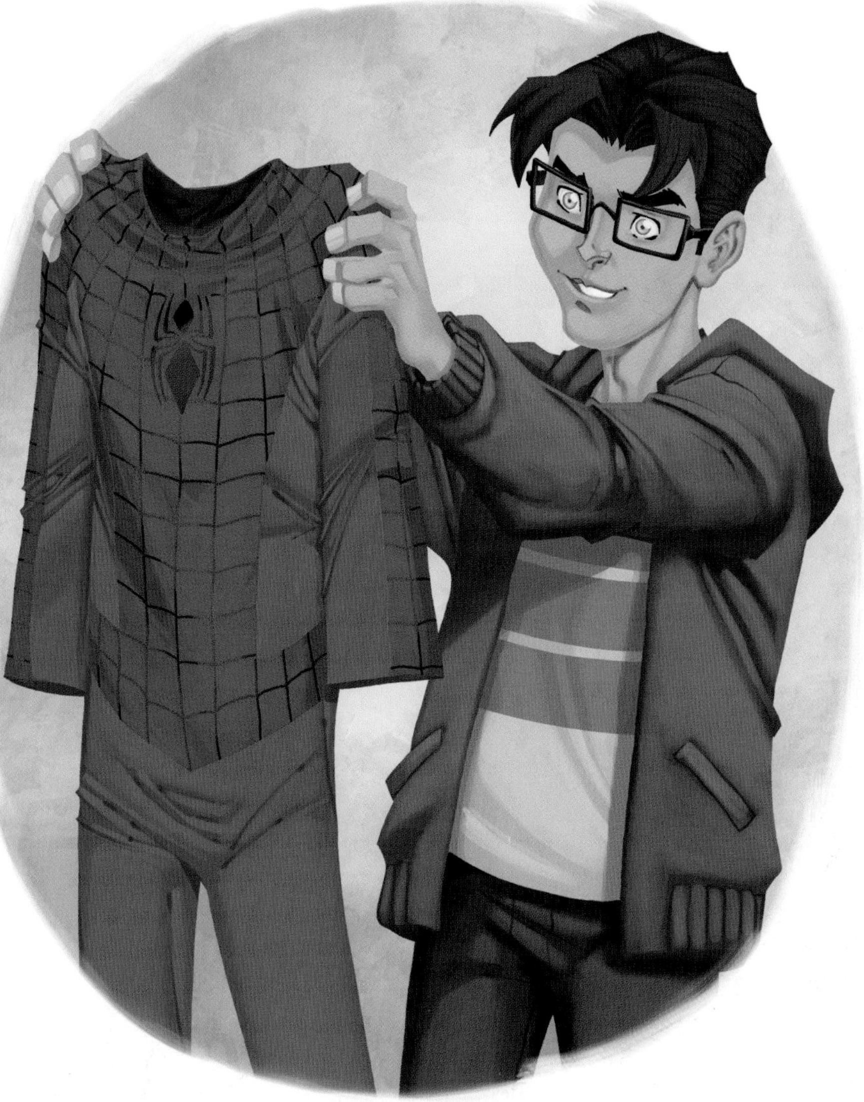

He has a costume.

He has web-shooters.

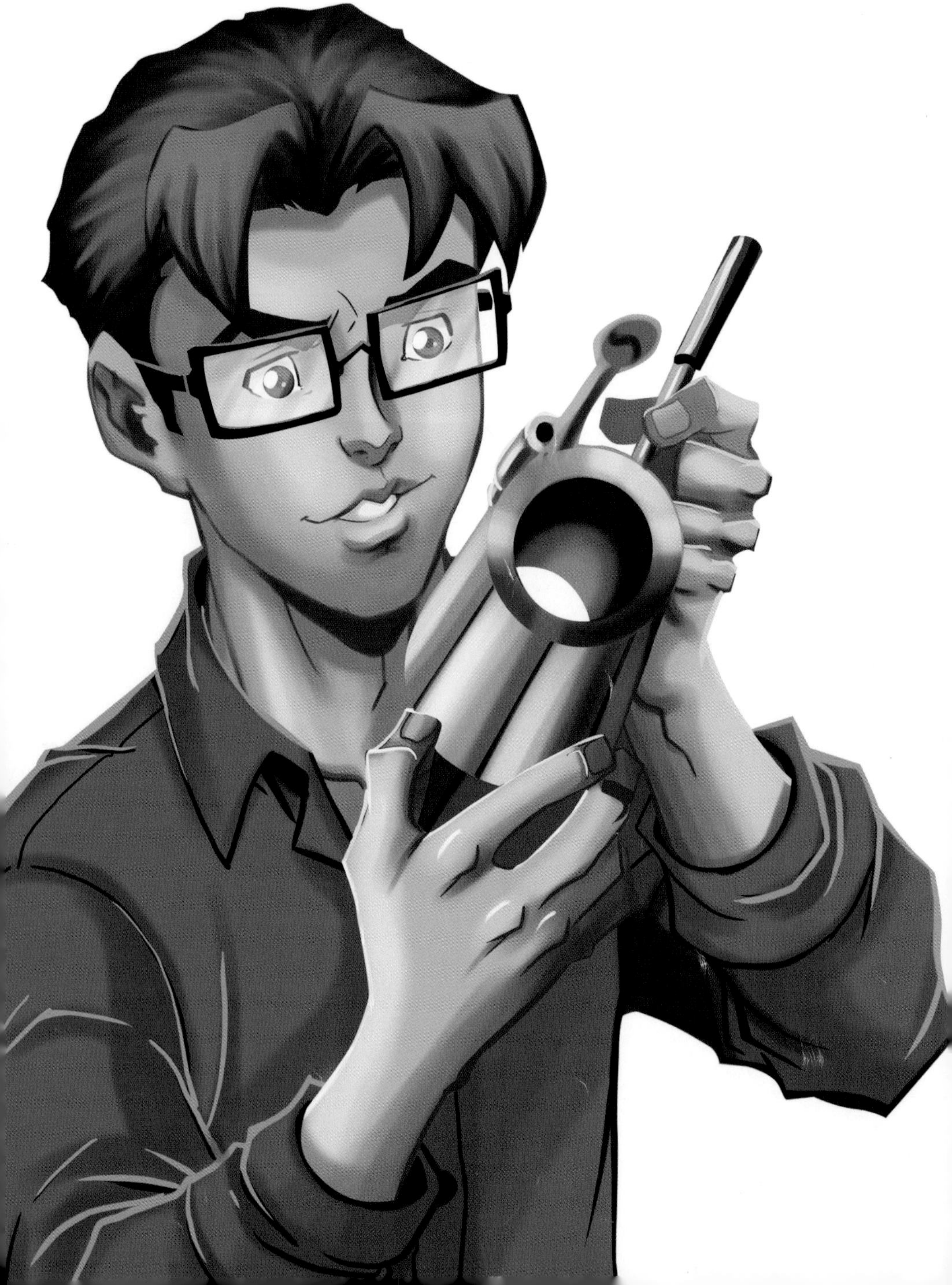

He makes webs.

He shoots webs.

This is his costume.
It has a spider on it.
It has webs on it, too.

Peter puts on his costume.
Peter has a secret name.

He calls himself
Spider-Man.

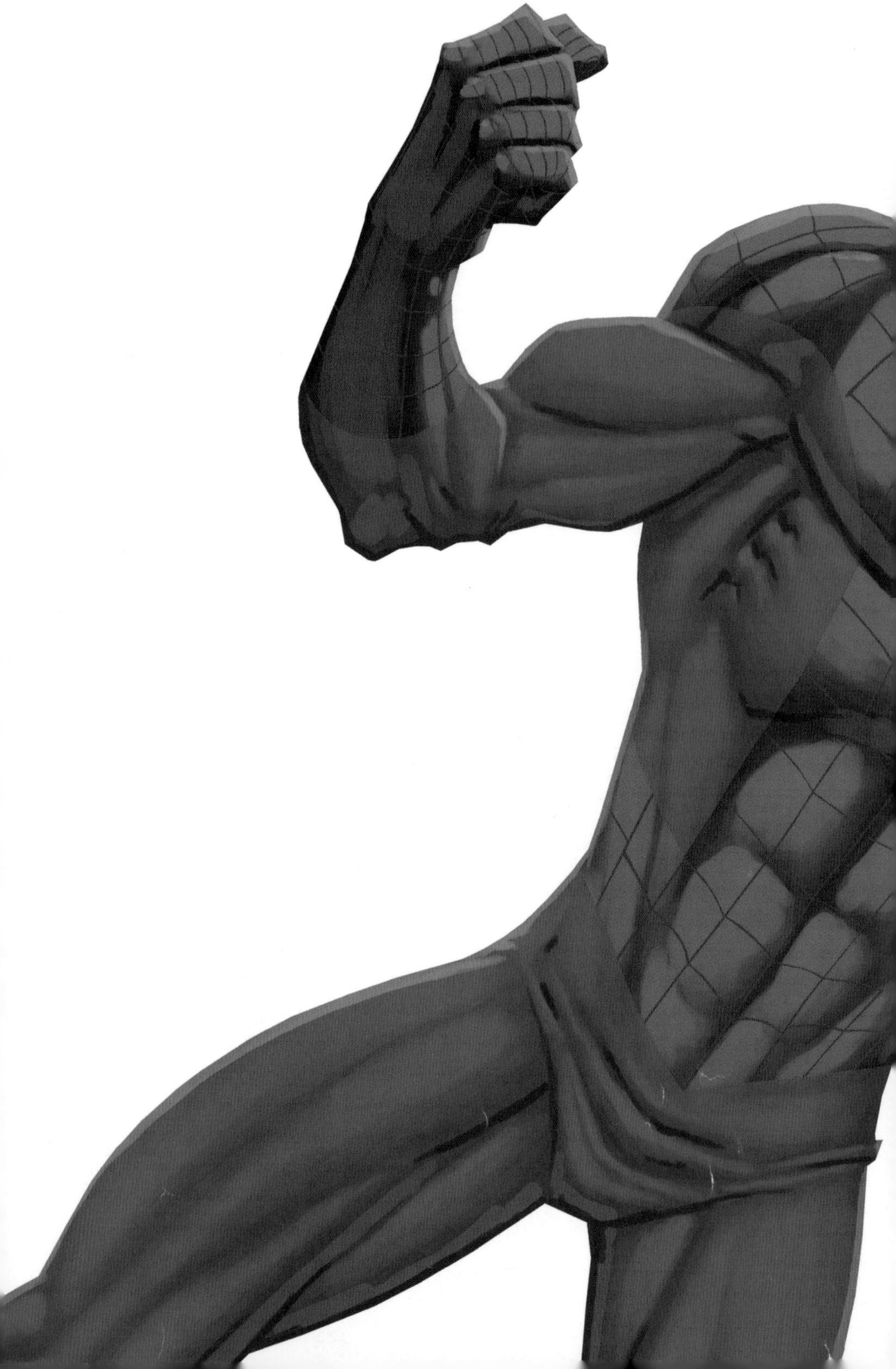

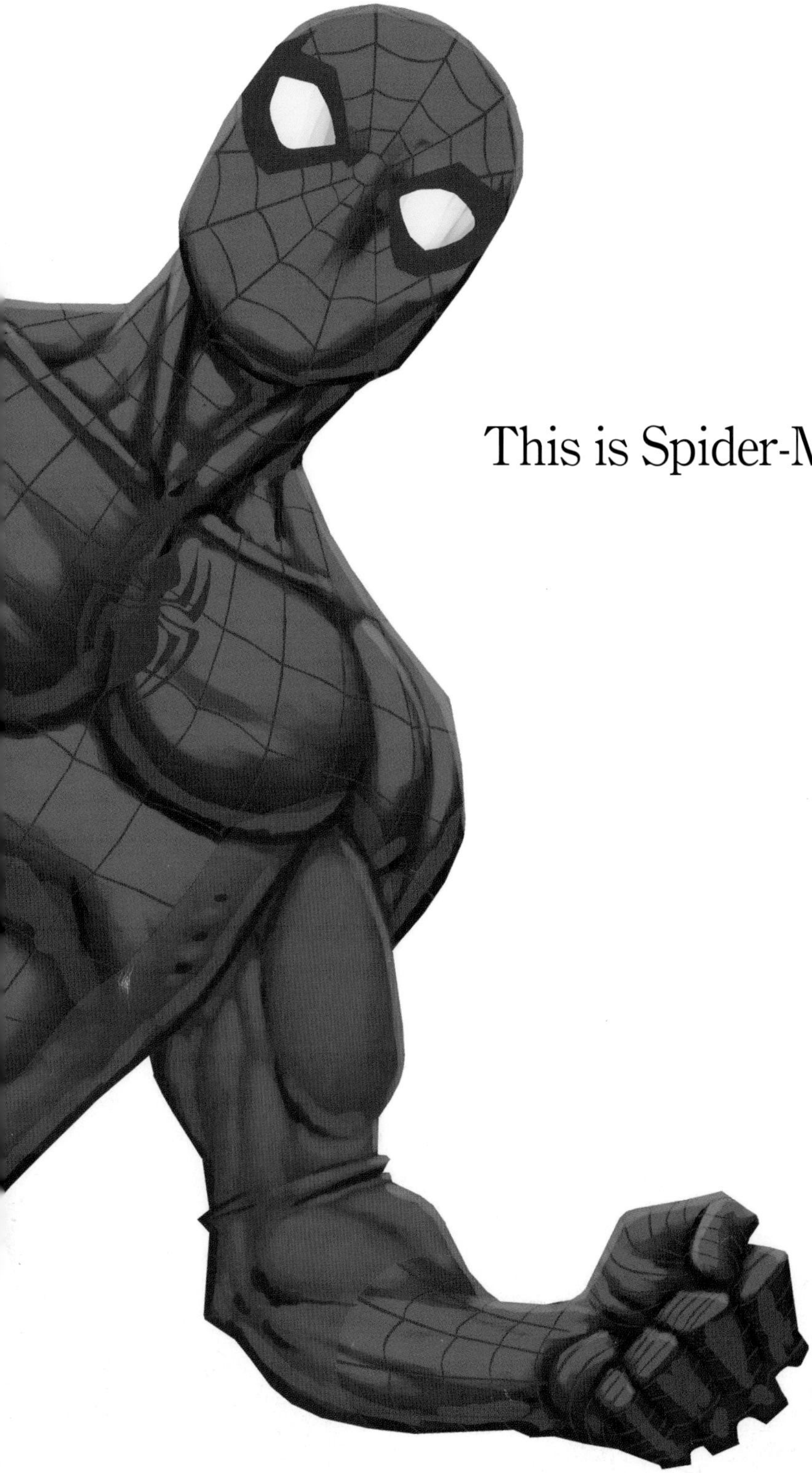

This is Spider-Man.

Spider-Man can climb
up walls.

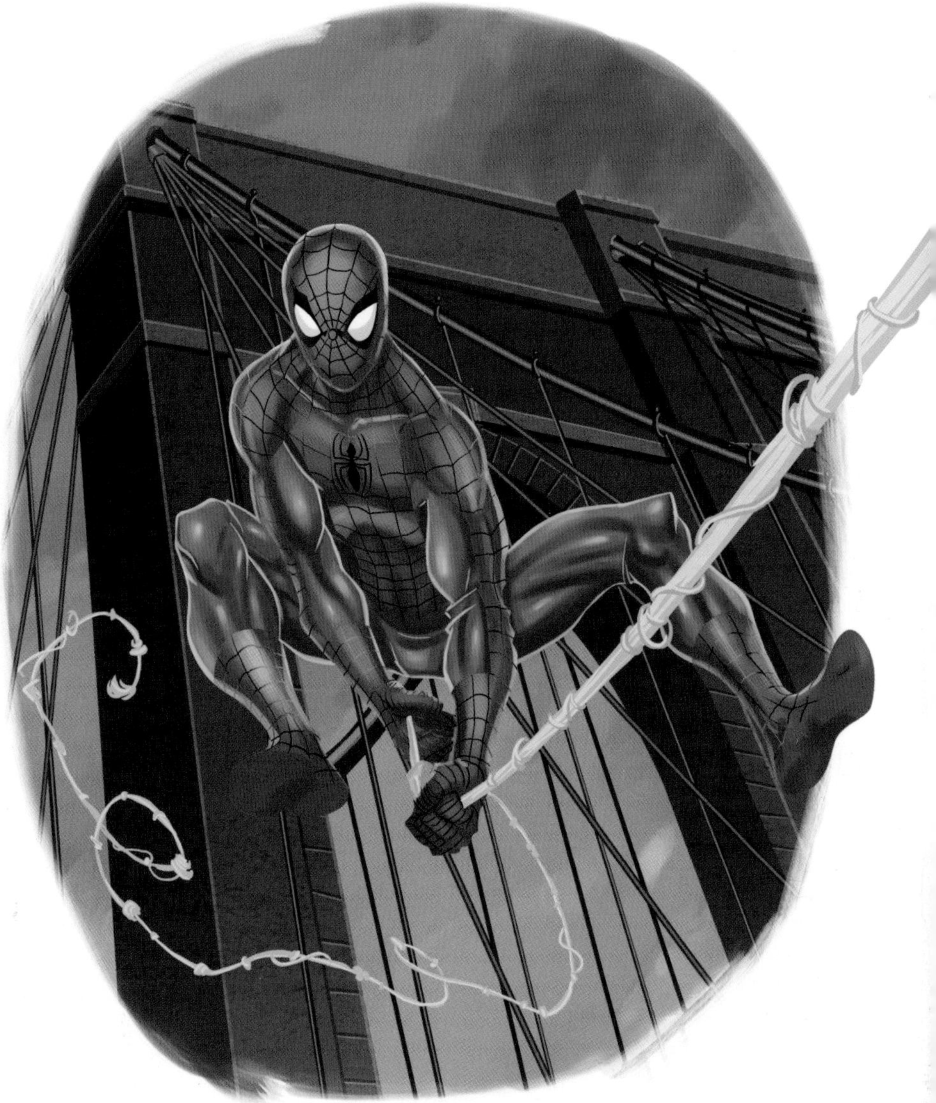

He can swing on
his webs.

He shoots his webs.

His webs stop bad guys.

Peter takes off his mask.
He is tired.

Peter goes to sleep.

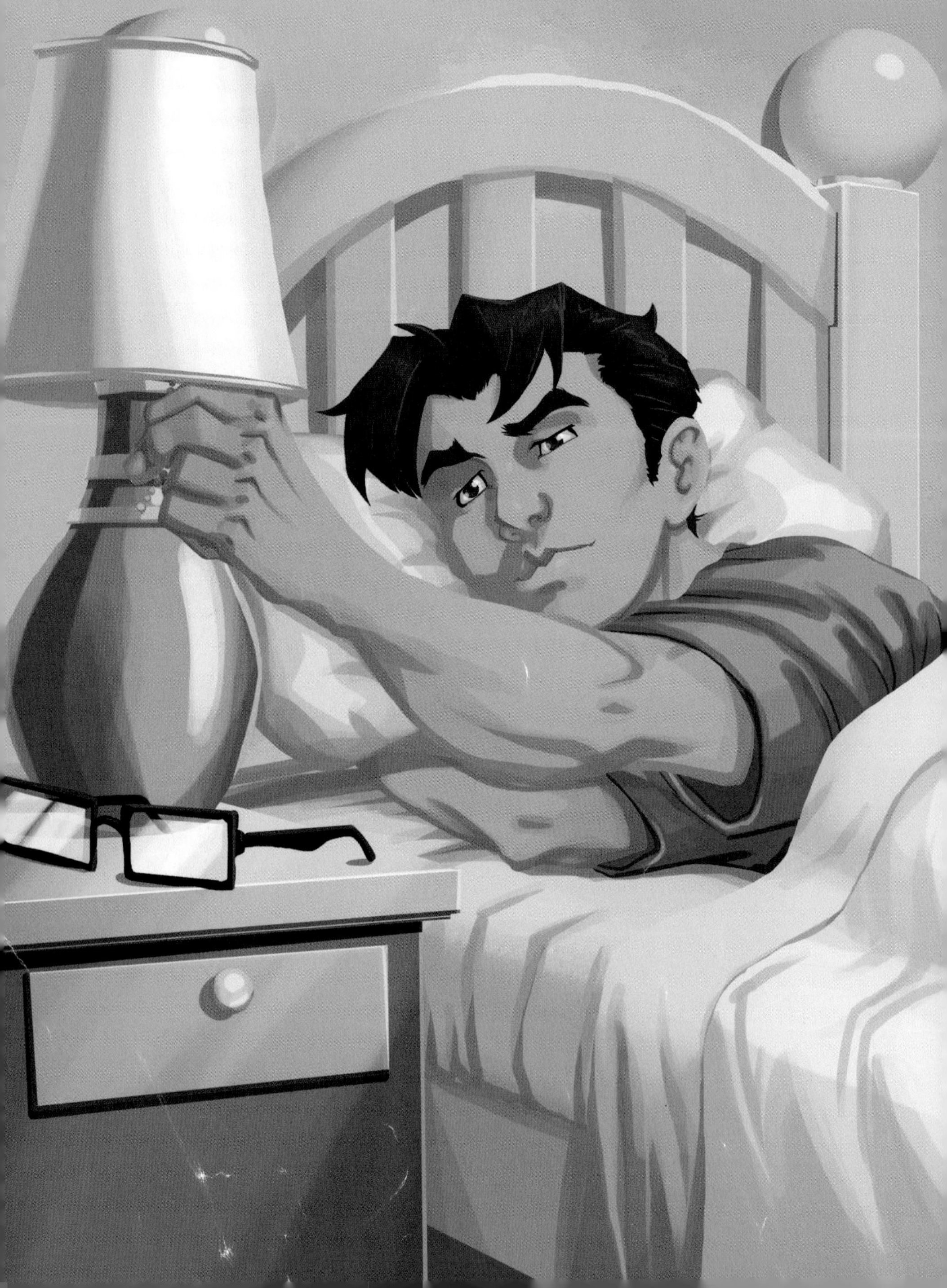

Peter wakes up. He gets
ready for school.

At school, the kids learn
about Spider-Man.

They like Spider-Man.

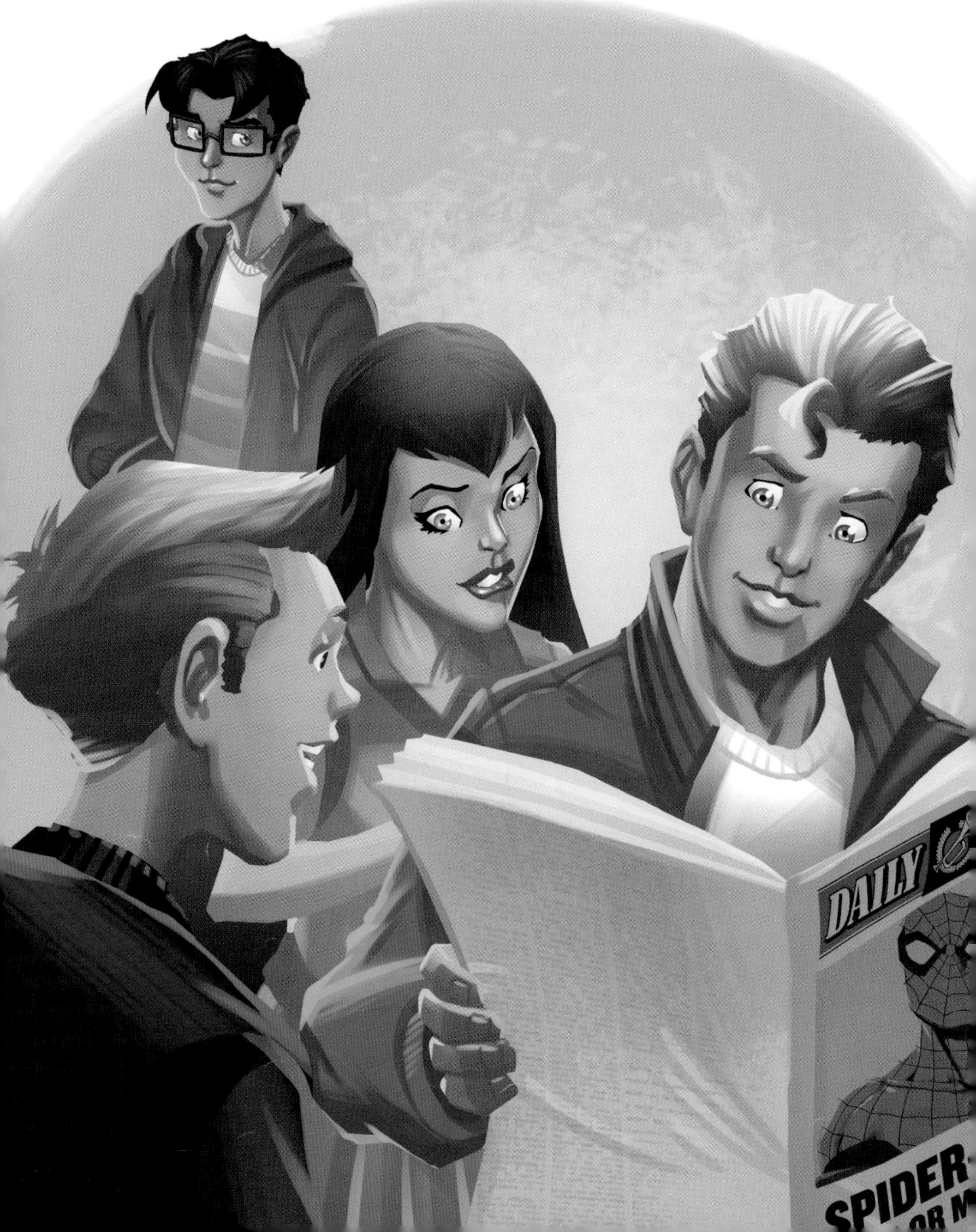
DAILY
SPIDER

They do not like Peter.

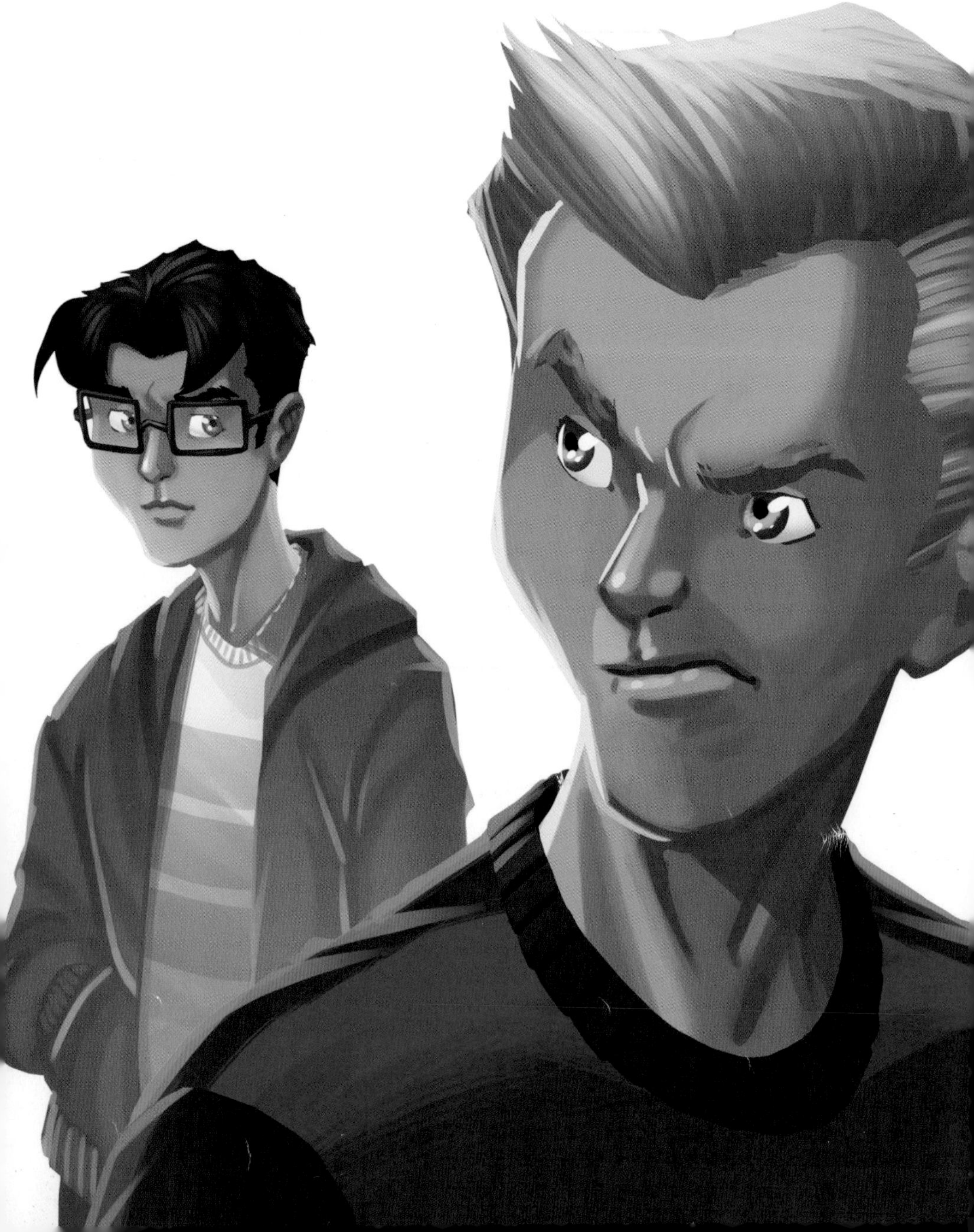

But they do not know
Peter's secret.

Peter is Spider-Man.

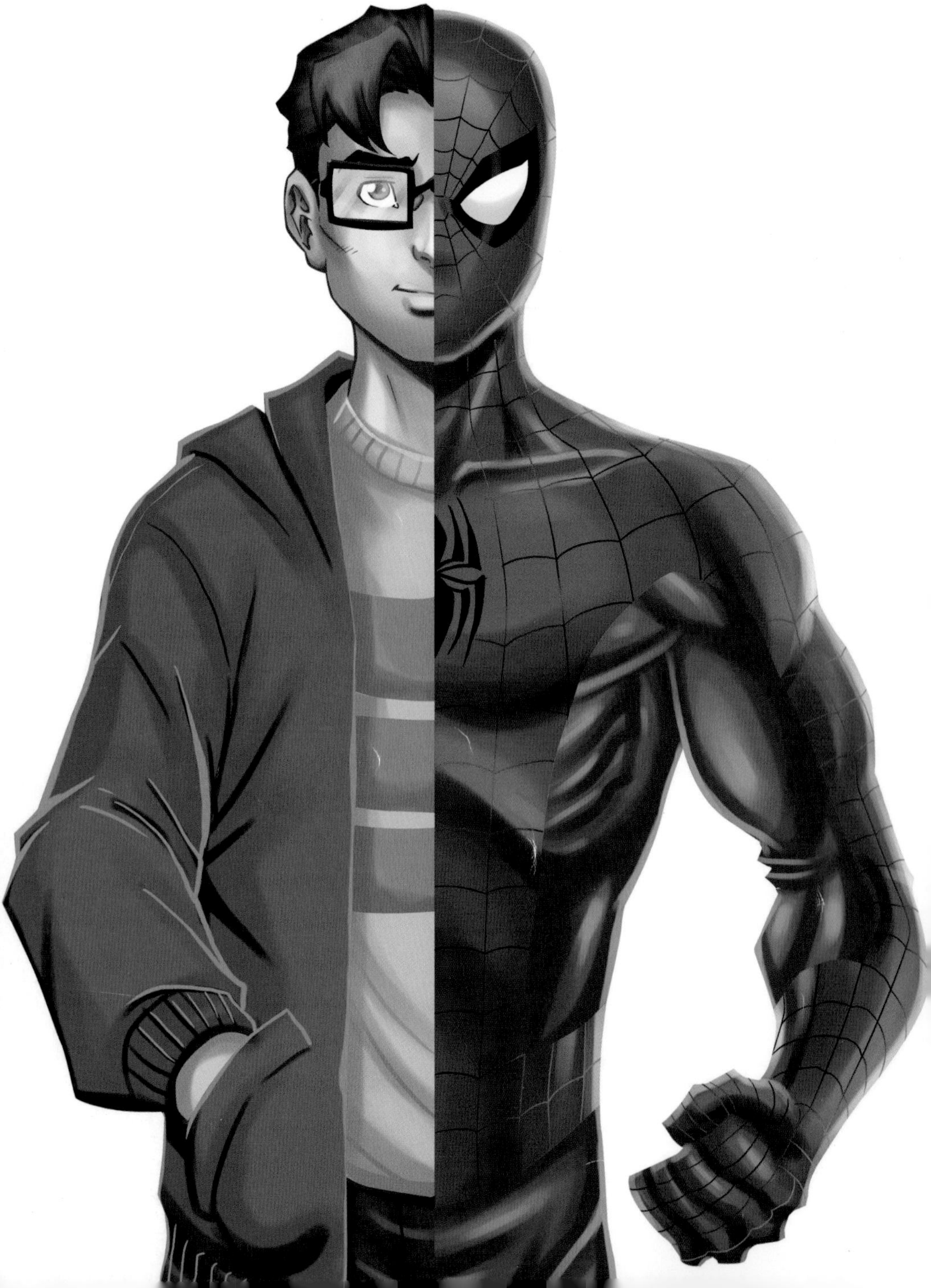